HAILMAN

OTHER TITLES FROM THE EMMA PRESS

POETRY PAMPHLETS

The Whimsy of Dank Ju-Ju, by Sascha Aurora Akhtar
Vivarium, by Maarja Pärtna, trans. from Estonian by Jayde Will
how the first sparks became visible, by Simone Atangana Bekono,
trans. from Dutch by David Colmer

SHORT STORIES

The Secret Box, by Daina Tabūna, trans. from Latvian by Jayde Will
Once Upon A Time In Birmingham, by Louise Palfreyman
Tiny Moons: A Year of Eating in Shanghai, by Nina Mingya Powles
Postcard Stories 2, by Jan Carson

POETRY ANTHOLOGIES

Everything That Can Happen: Poems about the Future
The Emma Press Anthology of Contemoprary Gothic Verse
The Emma Press Anthology of Illness

BOOKS FOR CHILDREN

Poems the wind blew in, by Karmelo C Iribarren,
tr. from Spanish by Lawrence Schimel
My Sneezes Are Perfect, by Rakhshan Rizwan
The Bee Is Not Afraid of Me: A Book of Insect Poems

POETRY AND ART SQUARES

The Goldfish, by Ikhda Ayuning Maharsi Degoul,
illustrated by Emma Wright
Menagerie, by Cheryl Pearson, illustrated by Amy Evans
One day at the Taiwan Land Bank Dinosaur Museum,
by Elīna Eihmane

hailman

Leanne Radojkovich

| |||| |||||

*For Julena Ciprian
and Ljubomir (Leo) Radojkovich*

ııııı

THE EMMA PRESS

First published in the UK in 2021 by the Emma Press Ltd.

Text © Leanne Radojkovich 2021.

All rights reserved.

The right of Leanne Radojkovich to be identified as the author of this work has been asserted in accordance with the Copyright, Designs and Patents Act 1988.

ISBN 978-1-912915-70-5

A CIP catalogue record of this book
is available from the British Library.

Printed and bound in the UK
by Imprint Digital, Exeter.

The Emma Press
theemmapress.com
hello@theemmapress.com
Birmingham, UK

CONTENTS

War Stories 1

Hailman 8

On Spinning 11

Double Dose 19

The Vilina Vlas Hotel 31

Missing 37

Cats and Dogs 51

Where the river meets the sea 65

Drive-by 77

Growing 86

Acknowledgements *94*

About the author *95*

About The Emma Press *96*

War Stories

There was no rain that summer and the heat was fierce. Trees were stripped to the bone. Pop's pet rose bush was a thorny crown in the centre of the parched lawn. Drought restrictions meant no watering. The sun turned the iron-roofed house into a sauna. Inside, Grandma was recovering from an operation. Pop and I sat in the carport hoping for a breeze. He ground his false teeth and gripped his *Best Bets* magazine like he was about to rip it in two. All day he drank beer. Sometimes he'd speak to an invisible person, crushing *Best Bets* into a ball. We could hear Grandma moan from the carport, and Mum responding in her soothing tone. Grandma would eventually doze off. Then we'd hear the squeak of the fridge door being opened for tonic; the freezer for just one ice cube – so the gin had more bite, said Mum.

Mum told me Pop had the beginnings of dementia and was experiencing magical thinking. He was stuck in an intense silence and my nose was stuck in a book. It was definitely not a time of magical chats.

Occasionally I'd be reading and hear a thud indoors. I'd look up to see Grandma's face at the bedroom window. She'd stare out at the bony trees, spellbound, until Mum helped her back into bed. In the evenings, I'd sit in Grandma's room reading aloud from the *Woman's Weekly*, including ads, and the *Herald*'s death notices. She'd rest her hand on my knee, whispering over and over 'Wonderful, wonderful,' a dab of glitter in each eye. Then Pop took over and spent the night in her room.

I dreamt of stagnation: oil slicks with fish drowning in them; me as a tortoise, slowly turning to stone. I didn't fight these dreams. I was too drained and felt strangely old, although I was only fourteen. Mum and I had gone to Pop and Grandma's for the summer holidays so we could help out. I had no friends in that town, and there were no laptops or cellphones back then. My sister stayed home. She'd left school the year before and was working in a bakery.

The library was two streets away and I had Grandma's card. Every few days I'd load up with thrillers and war stories: *The Medusa Touch, Catch-22,*

Kelly's Heroes. Pop had been in the war on the other side of the world. He was a kid at the time, and had no family left by the end. Grandma said Pop was lucky to survive, although not even she knew exactly what happened. Whenever I asked Pop about his childhood, he'd clack his false teeth and say he'd never had one.

My sister rang every couple of days to see how Grandma was doing. Then she'd ask about the 'old troll'. 'He's harmless now,' I'd reply. She and Pop had clashed from the start. Once, he tore down the paper doll chains we'd stuck to the lounge wall and ripped them up. For one long electric moment we'd gaped at him, then my sister punched his thigh and took off. 'Nothing should be sellotaped to wallpaper,' Grandma said afterwards, as a kind of explanation.

How carefully we'd smoothed flat those sheets of paper and folded them in half, then in half again. How carefully we'd drawn the outlines of the girls and snipped around, then lifted them out one after another, hand in hand, to dance around the room.

As summer wore on, Grandma grew more gaunt. She stopped wearing her wig – too hot. Pop stopped wearing his teeth, his mouth a sad pocket. The hiss when he pulled the tab off a can of beer. The clink of Mum's lonely ice cube.

I read book after book, skimming the lines until they turned into a kind of life raft. I read cereal boxes at breakfast, ingredient lists on biscuit packets and baked bean cans. We made our own food during the day, and must have had proper dinners together although I can't remember them.

Heat parboiled the air. It felt like we were hypnotised, walking down a dream hall, moving forward as if drawn along by a string. Bees floated past like dandelion seeds – I hadn't seen that before. Flies crouched everywhere, sizzling.

I thought Pop liked being in the carport with me – it wasn't just to escape the sauna of the house. I thought he liked my tortoise-stillness compared to his compressed energy that seemed to rise and boil up through his hair. 'Why are you always reading!' he burst out one afternoon. 'You don't have enough… stories… of your own?' His words crumbled. He smacked the book out of my hands. I picked it up off the concrete. 'Do you want me to read to you?' I asked. 'Grandma likes it when I read to her.' He shivered and stared at his hands.

Mum turned on the kitchen light. It turned the air outside amber. The rose bush glimmered as if wrapped in tinfoil. A few withered leaves still clung on but I wouldn't dare nip them off. The sky darkened. Stars opened. The rose bush disappeared in the deepening gloom. In that moment I saw my sister and me, hand in hand. Me wearing her old corduroy pinafore with ruffle straps and a sash tie. *Ring a ring a rosie*, we danced around the roses, *a pocket full of posies, A-tishoo! A-tishoo! We all fall down.* We thumped down and rolled onto our backs. The roses' scent above us was sweet and spicy, strong as incense. We looked at each other, then jumped up and ran our fingers across the fat velvety blooms. Petals slipped off and swivelled down in red splotches. Pop appeared. Slap! Slap! We stumbled back, cheeks scalded. 'I hate you, I hate you,' my sister sobbed and ran into the house, but I was stilled. We weren't allowed to touch his roses, yet I felt sure that wasn't why he'd struck us.

The hiss of Pop pulling the tab off a can of beer. The clink of Mum's lonely ice cube.

I stopped on my way from the house to the carport. I pressed the tip of my finger against a thorn on the rose bush. Blood welled from the puncture and I licked it off. I missed my sister. I wanted to leave school and get a job, too. We'd go flatting.

It was too early in the morning for Pop to join me. When I sat down I noticed an eerie lack of birdcalls. No sparrows fossicked the dry ground. No mynahs shrieked from the telegraph wires. It was so quiet I heard an inner thrum, like when you've had a fright or been running a long time and your heartbeat drums in your ears. I stared down at the piles of war books and thrillers on the concrete. The smell of pine trees wafted toward me, although there were none in the neighbourhood and the Christmas tree was long gone. For some reason I prickled with cold. My vision blurred then resolved. I saw a field of snow smooth as a sheet of paper. A shadow of a large bird slowly crossed the white ground and I felt myself sinking.

The afternoon Grandma died, the daylight dimmed. Clouds rolled in and everything turned grey and smelled of nails.

Pop and I were in the carport, while inside the house Mum made arrangements on the phone.

I was crushed. I couldn't read. Beside me, Pop

had shrunk like a week-old balloon, all his static gone. He held a can of beer but forgot to open it. I had the feeling he was only just there, now Grandma was gone; a puff of wind could have blown him away. I looked down and blinked back tears.

There was a bottomless silence where even the flies had stopped sizzling. The smell of pines grew strong. An image appeared. Two girls about six years old, holding hands. A spill of sunlight, a dazzling expanse of snow. Then a close-up: their hands were roped together. My heart shrank to a pinprick and a metallic taste rushed into my mouth. Their chests torn from gunshots. Pop, about twelve, a gun hanging from one hand, a soldier behind him with a pistol to his head.

Hailman

| | (|| ||| | ||

Mum and I caught the bus to visit Aunty Joyce on Saturday mornings. Joyce wasn't my real Aunty; I just called her that out of manners. Whenever we visited, she was mending or making gowns for ballroom dancing – liquid fabrics, shimmering falls of sequins. She'd talk with pins in the side of her mouth, and when the pins ran out she'd fit a cigarette into a holder and light up. She let me play with her offcuts. I'd feel her glances. *If looks could kill...* Of course they couldn't, but they could brush against the back of your neck; they could caress your cheek.

The last time we went, it was winter. The cold made ringworms on my thighs, and there were huge sooty clouds overhead that crashed and sparked. We got out of the bus and hurried to Joyce's. I held Mum's hand tight. We waited on the porch, the temperature plunging between one knock and the next. There was a strange hush, as if the clouds were sucking up air, and then hail shot down. The smell of knives burst from the concrete path. The door opened and Mum pushed me inside. Hail crackled against the windows. Joyce dashed down the hall and opened the back door. Pellets popped and clumped onto the patio. I squeezed past her and crouched down to touch the magic I'd never seen before (I'd never seen snow either).

'Come back,' Mum called.

'Let her enjoy it.' Joyce crouched beside me. We were both getting wet; her mascara smudged and a crumb dribbled down her face in a black tear.

Joyce and I began squashing hail into a mound until there was a soccer ball. 'It needs a head,' she said. We scooped together a smaller ball and plonked it on top.

'A snowman!' I squealed. 'A hailman!' I snapped off dandelion flowers for eyes and a geranium twig for a nose. Joyce pulled brass buttons from her pocket and poked them into the face, and the hailman smiled. I watched her hands, the same as mine: narrow, fingers slim as chopsticks. Her wrists had the same bony knob on the side. I felt queasy and leant against the wall.

Joyce felt my gaze and caught it. Her pale eyes

darkened. They made me think of the steel mirrors in school loos where all you can see is your shadow. She stood up and whisked down the hall. Mum tried to pull me inside, but I wouldn't leave the hailman. The popping stopped and turned into rain. The hailman began melting – half his body sheared away and the head rolled off. Soon he was only a puddle. I picked up the brass buttons and slipped them into my pocket.

On Spinning

A storm hit in the night, terracotta pots crashing across the deck. There was a tremendous crack followed by a tearing sound and a thump, and the raw scent of foliage shot through the gap between window and sill. The curtains lifted in waves over my head; I rolled to the far side of the bed. Earlier, I'd listened to a woman who'd escaped from a cult being interviewed on the radio. She'd floated like a spider's thread, she said, settling in a caravan park in Brisbane. I'd been sorting my clothes into piles and only half-listening until then. 'I didn't want to leave my younger brothers behind. That was the hardest part: going alone, in the middle of the night, knowing I might never see them again.' I was about to make a similar journey across the sea, except my brother had left me.

The next morning was calm. Gulls silently circled overhead and sparrows hopped across the lawn. A branch had torn off the gum tree; I dragged it over to the fence. The silver leaves gleamed – hard to believe they'd been dying for hours. Then I caught the scent of a neighbouring pine and flashed back to the day I'd thrown buckets of hot water and disinfectant down the dogshit-encrusted path to my old family home.

I'd been so mad at my brother Brent, his face frosted with stubble, ash-blonde hair sticking up as if conducting static – he looked as calcified as those turds. The house had always been a tip, so I should have expected it, but he had to be out in three days and nothing was packed. His dog had died a week before and the body was still under a tarp: 'What's the point of burying him? The bulldozers will do it.'

Brent had lived in our house his whole life. All the yards in the street backed onto bush, with paths beaten between. There were cricks and bells of birds all year round, and a mazy hum of mosquitoes in summer. A creek lay at the bottom. It was more of a raggedy line of puddles, and when rain came the puddles joined up and eels slipped through like shadows.

By the time I was seven we'd buried in the bush two canaries, a guinea pig and a cat. Brent and I wanted to put Mum there too, so she'd stay close.

Dad said no: there was a special place for people and that's where Mum would go. Brent was such a sweet little boy. I loved him like a teddy. He'd stood there quietly, wearing his toy sword and pirate hat, then he touched Dad's hand. 'You need a lie-down, Daddy,' he said, and led him back to the house.

Later we wrapped up Mum's heart earrings and a macaroni necklace Brent had made at kindy, put them in a baking powder tin and buried them under the flax. Then we rocked back on our haunches looking up to heaven. Had Mum seen? We couldn't tell.

I remembered Brent and Dawn in the sunshine two years later. He held up a bird's nest shimmering with strands of his platinum hair and her orange lengths. She'd decorated the nest for his treasures: a broken cup with the Queen's face on it, a kingfisher feather, a teaspoon in the shape of a cockle shell. He hugged Dawn's thigh as tightly as he'd hugged Mum's, and she called him her human caliper.

Memories like these eddy like autumn leaves. Dawn blowing into our lives – her parents wanted her to have a fresh start and Dad said sure, she could stay and look after the kids while he was at work.

Dawn had a mass of carroty hair, big as a bonfire. Her father had the same fiery hair. When he put his arm around her and squeezed goodbye, her face greyed. After her parents left, Dawn picked up Brent and swirled him around the kitchen, singing 'These Boots Are Made for Walking'. She wore a jingly charm anklet and a toe ring, and cooked purple-dyed spaghetti sauce and cheese omelettes stuffed with popcorn. Brent and I weren't sure whether Dawn was a child or a grown-up. She smoked stinky rollies, and after a while Dad did too. She had a lazy eye which would swivel to the left when she smoked – I never quite knew where she was looking. Then she got fat and five months later had twins.

In the meantime Brent and I played in the bush. I made forts along the creek's edge, with moats where I floated newspaper boats before letting them free on the current. Brent spent hours watching spiders spin webs. He kept still as a rock, because if you moved a millimetre the spider would stop mid-weave. On foggy mornings the bush glimmered with dew-strung webs. There were so many, hundreds connected with strands of spider silk, that we couldn't move without breaking one. At first Brent thought stars had fallen off the sky.

Sometimes we glimpsed a rat slinking between grassy toetoe skirts. Dead rats stunk for a week. We wondered how many bones were in the ground under our feet. Not just our old pets, but those rats, birds, skinks. Sometimes Brent dug holes searching for skulls and skeletons.

Carroty-haired babies came home from hospital squawking like ducks. 'Colic,' said the Plunket nurse. She made notes in her book and asked lots of questions. 'Have you any family support, dear?' The nurse came the next day and the one after that. A few weeks later Dad said he was bloody well going deaf. The nurse said it was time Dawn's parents came down. When the nurse left, Dawn squatted in a corner of the sofa, rocking.

After Dawn arrived, Brent and I had moved to bunk beds in my room. We had a big section and Dad, who was a builder, said he'd add another room. Dawn said she'd plant a garden and grow grapes, herbs, sunflowers. Then they got stuck into smoking pot and nothing happened. After a while, Dawn planted a tomato garden behind the house. The plants grew huge, with leaves the size of dinner plates – but no tomatoes. She pulled out the plants and hung them upside down in the garage.

When I arrived at our old house, the spoon and rubber tie had fallen to the floor and Brent was slumped, eyes wide, face stretched back as if he were tearing past on his motorbike. He was scrawny and ill-looking. I knelt beside him and put my head against his arm. I felt so tender, now that my anger had rolled away down the path along with those dog turds.

    I remembered the day Dawn breathed dope smoke over the babies' squinched-up faces until they nodded off. Her lazy eye swivelled and she glared at us – so blazed her eye was almost out on a stalk – then she stomped into the bathroom and locked the door. Brent and I waited to see what happened next. We heard Dawn crack open the window, then nothing. She didn't come out for ages. Maybe she'd fallen asleep in there? I made peanut butter and jam sandwiches and we crept out of the house, going as far as we could to the tallest trees. There was a strange silence: no breeze in leaves, no birds whistling. We sat on a thick carpet of moss. The night before, the babies had cried and cried while Dawn and Dad shouted at each other about her parents coming down. Brent had climbed into my bunk and we'd lain together, shivering. The next day, sleep-deprived, we sat quietly on the moss mechanically eating our sandwiches, crumb by crumb.

Something thumped on the ground. We got up to see what it was – Dawn's sneaker. A creak overhead, then we looked up and saw her dangling.

I made Brent and me a cup of tea and sat on the back step as the sun sank. 'Come and look,' I said. He shuffled across from the sofa. The sun was a fat orange honey-ball, its rays turning the flax spears into flaming green swords. I saw a crescent moon hanging low in the sky and I don't know why but I started crying. Brent squeezed down beside me and I sniffed back tears. Birds hooted in dark trees and swallows swept across the deepening blue.

'Come to Aussie with me,' I said. 'We'll have fun exploring.'

'Nah, I'm sorted.'

'Where are you going?'

'A mate's farm.'

'What mate?'

'You don't know him.'

'Then come over for a holiday. Promise?'

'Sure, why not.'

I put my head on his bony shoulder and we watched faraway stars. 'I love you, Cassie,' he said, and then I cried buckets. It was the first time he'd said that.

It was foggy when he left the property three days later. The fog may have played a part, police said. His motorbike crossed the centre line and collided with a milk tanker.

I went back a month later. All the houses in our street had been trucked off site, trees chopped down, the creek diverted and filled in. Bulldozers had left a smooth brown field, and new sections were marked out with gossamer-like string, taut as the frame lines of a web.

I stood on the kerb thinking of everything in that soil: Mum's earrings and macaroni necklace, Dawn's sneaker, childhood pets, Brent's dog.

New houses and families would come. The earth would gather in their offerings too.

Double Dose

A teenager riding an e-scooter shot across the intersection towards Patsy. She stepped aside, the front wheel took the kerb sideways, and the scooter spun out from under him. He cracked headfirst onto the footpath and blood sprayed out. He's dead, Patsy thought, and squatted beside him. A man wearing a face mask ran over the road – 'Don't touch him.' The boy groaned and foam trickled out of his mouth. She sat back. 'Ring 111,' the man said, as he dragged off his jacket and laid it across the boy's chest. She was shaking and couldn't tap in the numbers. He pulled out his phone and dialled. A dog rounded the corner and sniffed at the boy's shoulder; Patsy shoved it away. 'Help's on the way,' she told the boy quietly. 'Just hold on, hold on.'

The ambulance drove onto the footpath. She rose and almost fainted. Pain shot through her lower abdomen; squatting had been a mistake. She watched until the ambulance disappeared – it felt as if part of her had gone with it. Then she turned and continued down the hill to catch her train.

Patsy's oldest friend, Sharon, had called the day before and asked her to come down: 'I'm going crazy in this shit town.' Sharon had flown in from Aussie because her dad had died and she was sorting out his house and cremation. Her brother was stuck in Brisbane with a sick kid, so it was all up to her. She spoke without drama – she'd always been matter of fact – and Patsy, who'd recently had surgery and wasn't meant to drive, said, 'Sure, I'll come for the weekend.'

A woman wearing a polka-dot face mask entered the carriage first. She and Patsy were the only passengers; trains were still running but no-one knew for how long. Patsy waited for the woman to choose her seat. She wondered about putting on her mask, then didn't. She had disposable ones from the chemist, which reminded her of hospitals and made her feel claustrophobic. The woman settled on the back seat and pulled a cap low across her brow so only a finger-width of eye showed. Patsy sat at the front, the maximum possible distance apart, although it was way more than required. She tried to remember: did they have to be one metre apart, or two? The rules kept morphing, but face masks were not yet compulsory.

The train to her home town had been reinstated a month ago, after being mothballed for 30 years. She and Sharon used to laugh about it being a hillbilly village. As teenagers they'd taken the train up to the real city for a concert, a night largely lost to drugs and booze. They'd bought the cheapest seats, at the top of the stadium's amphitheatre – so far away from the stage that the band, when they came on, were like ants. A guitar note spangled out and the audience in the centre gelled into a massive anemone, their raised arms wavering hairs. It was only much later, in the petri dish of memory, that the tiny band members expanded into the mane-tossing glory of the posters on her bedroom wall.

The carriage doors slid together. The train moved slowly past the platform then accelerated. The backs of shops flickered by: a mural of squirrels hopping from building to building; wire fencing with rubbish blown into the diamonds; blowsy late-summer fennel grown man-high. The sky was a pure, surgical blue. Patsy rested her head against the window. The night before she'd taken Tramadol and, despite sleeping well, her mind floated… She thought of the boy on the footpath, blood pooling around his head. She thought of the oxygen mask pressed over her face. 'Relax, now count backwards from ten' – and bliss spiralled up.

She woke at midday, the sun burning white. She shaded her eyes and gazed at the countryside passing by. Summer-crisp paddocks stretched to a craggy mountain range in the distance. The train crossed the bridge over the river. She'd swum in that river, swung across on willow fronds, sat beside it at night smoking and gossiping with school friends. She'd tried to run from it, once – but the river's muddy edge snared her ankle and she'd dropped like the boy from that morning. Her stomach cramped.

The train pulled into a stop. A father and son stepped into the carriage. The son, aged about eight, had a toy rifle slung across his shoulder. 'Morning,' Patsy said as they walked by. The father gave her a nod and sat precisely in the middle. The son pointed the gun at her behind his father's back and pulled the trigger, then sent her a shy, angelic grin. She smiled at him. Her heart turned into air.

The train trembled then slid out of the station. She saw her reflection in the window: her dress was unbleached linen, ghostly on the glass, and the square neckline seemed to emphasise how prominent her collarbones had become.

They passed more parched paddocks with cows sitting still as rocks beneath ancient alder trees. The old factory's smokestacks appeared. The factory had shut long ago, and rusting iron sheets covered windows and doors. Her father had worked there. Each morning her mother made him a packed lunch and thermos of tea and they'd pecked each other's cheeks goodbye. Her father had made it to 63 and her mother to 49, the same age she was now. A hawk rose above the smokestacks, light as ash, slowly circling higher on a thermal.

The carriage doors opened and Patsy stepped onto an extended, renovated platform – sleek and modern and unrecognisable from her childhood. Her trolley bag purred along the smooth concrete path then clackety-clacked along the pitted tarseal footpath outside. Her step quickened as she approached the maze of streets and cul-de-sacs; everything seeming smaller than she remembered. She stopped outside her old home. Wooden venetian blinds lined the windows where net curtains had moved in the breeze.

She remembered the grandfather clock's asthmatic tick-tick and rickety chime on the hour. *Like sands through the hourglass...* she'd heard a million times on TV, intoned as if a priest were reading scripture. Her mother had watched every episode in a swoon. 'Muuum... Muuum!' a child called from the back of the property. Patsy moved on. Heat shimmied up from the footpath, and tears blurred her vision. She wiped her eyes.

The bus shelter was just up ahead. She and Sharon used to scramble down the bank behind it to the river. A boardwalk had been built across the bank and a circular lookout looped around. She crossed the road and walked out to the farthest point. The river's pickled tang sheeted up; she hadn't smelt that fragrance for years. Muscular currents were braiding and unbraiding, relentless – even in the shallows she could see the water slithering through stones, hissing with busyness. One afternoon, she'd stared at the river until it was no longer an expanse of water: it was a creature, a vast eel with rippling skin. She'd been frightened of eels ever since. Sharon would freak her out by saying they oozed out of the river at night and climbed up the bank to her house. Once, Patsy found a dead elver, its body a leathery sock and its eye a pecked-out hole. 'What kills little eels?' she asked her father. 'Bigger ones,' he'd laughed.

A broken-off branch sailed past and its wake glittered, slicing like memory, like the eyes of the hatchlings. She'd been swinging off a tree branch when it had snapped and a nest smashed to the ground. Pairs of sun-pricked eyes stared up at her. She should have put them out of their misery; instead she'd turned to stone as life twitched out of them. The mother bird circled the tree shrieking until night fell. Another, deeper memory of sharp eyes began to slice through. Patsy spun away. The sun was so strong against her back that she felt X-rayed. She was a glass eel, as she'd said when the doctor showed her the image of her organs, clearly defined in a gin-coloured body.

She pulled her trolley bag across the road and headed to Sharon's. A skip was parked on the verge outside: it was full, the legs of an upside-down chair poking out. Huge orange cosmos plants grew in the front garden, stalks spidering out in all directions like tumbleweeds.

The door opened and there she was, looking

just the same and completely different. They stood there smiling at each other. Then Sharon put her arms around her and lifted her off her feet. 'Make yourself at home,' she said. 'I'll make a pot of tea.'

The lounge was empty except for a sofa, a coffee table and a TV sitting on a beer crate. It was hot, yet all the windows were open. The Phoenix palm at the end of the section had mushroomed in size. A starling disappeared into a cavity at the top of the trunk – it reminded Patsy of sneaking out at night with Sharon. They'd fit themselves into the hollows and gaps of hedges and fences and creep to the end of the road. In winter they'd slip into the bus shelter, just to have their own space. In summer they'd climb down the bank to the river. The water whooshed past while they sat around telling porno jokes about their teachers or the deputy principal – his mad frizz of hair, how he strutted around the grounds like a rooster nursing haemorrhoids. Miss Clarke, the ancient office lady who pencilled on eyebrows in a cartoon arch of surprise; her cherry lipstick. At home, Patsy's mother was coughing up blood, and Patsy had told no one, not even Sharon. Such a ridiculous idea, that not speaking about it would dial down the reality. Her mother's rattly breathing in the night hurt her heart, same as the rat that gasped its last beneath the kitchen floorboards one morning. Did rats cry? Did they have souls? In the silence that followed, she'd felt the dead rat's presence in the crawlspace beneath her feet.

She was beginning to ebb. She placed her hand on the windowsill so as not to lose balance.

Sharon came in carrying a tray loaded with mugs, a teapot and a cake still in the supermarket wrapping. 'I spent all morning baking this for you.'

'Just a little, then,' Patsy said.

Sharon carved off a large slice. 'You look like you need a decent feed.'

How to say she couldn't eat? That everything tasted of metal? Patsy took the plate and a fork and placed them on the armrest. 'This is like my first flat I think that's the same beer crate!'

'Dad was a real hoarder. I've filled three skips since I've been here. Never threw out a nail, or a pair of shoes. Want a smoke? I gave up, but coming here made me start again.' Sharon went to the kitchen and returned with a packet, then drew out two cigarettes, lit them both and held one out.

'Probably shouldn't…' Patsy took a small puff. It made her dizzy.

'We had our first in the bus shelter,' Sharon said. 'You stole them from your mum.'

'I'd forgotten that.'

'Did you see the tip's gone? It's a farm now. Cows grazing on top of our rubbish. It's enough to put you off milk.'

'I saw cows at the old factory. They were wandering around where the big floral clock used to be.' She was functioning close to normal, thought Patsy, or perhaps that was an illusion? Her vision blurred again. She stubbed out her smoke in a saucer. A cow was drawn on the saucer – no – a horse.

'Let's go for a wander – see what else has changed,' said Sharon. 'Can't climb down to the river anymore. Did you see the boardwalk? Remember that time we thought the police were after us for smoking pot and we all took off, but you went the other way and we lost you? You were so lucky.'

'Yeah,' Patsy agreed flatly.

'Hey, are you ok? You look a bit pale.'

'I'm not feeling too great. Could I just lie down for a bit?'

'Of course. Come with me.' Sharon led Patsy to her brother's old room. It contained a single bed and a chair. 'Can I get you anything?'

'No, it's just the heat. I'll be ok.'

Sharon closed the door behind her and Patsy listened to her jandals slap down the hall.

She never thought she'd be staying in the brother's bedroom. It was a cold, shocking sensation, but she had to lie down and couldn't protest when so much was unspeakable.

Sharon's brother had been high on more than pot and beer the night he came to the river. He seemed knife-sharp, and paced the small beach while everyone else sat around passing joints. Sharon said he'd turned up the Saturday before at three in the morning, punched a hole through their front door.

There were seven of them and he was the eighth. It was a sticky evening, and screaming cicadas clasped the stalks of threadbare toetoe. Sharon told a long story about Miss Clarke's eyebrows. Patsy had been too stoned to grasp the punchline and laughed along to fit in. A police siren began howling and everyone jumped up. Her ankle turned in the mud and she fell back. When she sat up, the others had disappeared – except for him, his eyes glinting. Her chest tightened. She tried to stand, but her twisted ankle couldn't take the weight. She hopped ahead on her other leg: two hops, then she lost her balance on the squishy mud and crumpled again.

With terrible confidence he was on top of her. He pulled down the straps of her tank top with his teeth and bit her neck. She froze. The stink of him, his scraggly hair smothering her face.

Afterwards, she pretended it didn't happen, while at the same time she had perfect recall. Lately at night she'd started to feel his stinking breath and the shock of what happened, and she'd reach for the Tramadol. No need to suffer, the doctor had said; that much they could help with. She pulled a sachet of pills from her pocket and swallowed a double dose: one for pretending, one for remembering.

She had a sense of falling apart very slowly until all her feelings had oozed out. She observed her breath, the impersonal functioning of body parts, then that focus drained away too. The doctor had said it might end soon, or it might not.

The Vilina Vlas Hotel

I am haunted by a picture taken of my mother the last time I saw her. She kneels beside the lake feeding a swan, the bird's neck curving to her open hand. My aunt had some photos from those days in a suitcase beneath her bed, but we could never find this one. Sometimes I wondered if that photo had ever existed, or if it was something imprinted in my memory by the force of what happened next: *gunshot, a man crumpling onto the grass. My aunt slapped her hand across my eyes, pulling me to the ground. Her heart beat against my head – how it rushed, like a creek after rain.*

I don't remember what my mother said when we went to the airport. I can't remember her face, just her back as she knelt to that swan in the park and the blood-orange roses appliquéd to her coat. Yet I remember the plane's interior in minute detail: black leather piping around the seats, a fold-out table with a groove to hold my cup, the doll's house-sized windows. I remember the plane's rocky motion down the runway, the sudden thrust – a giant's hand pushing me into the clouds; then looking down on the tiled roofs of a toy town sloping away, minarets fine as pins on a pincushion, mountains like bumps in a rug.

I was seven years old. My mother didn't come with us because she was looking after Grandad, who was old and sick. My aunt took me – until things settled down. War came days later; soon after that Grandad was killed and my mother disappeared. My aunt and I waited for news, fourteen thousand kilometres away. Then it came: Mum had died in an accident. Weeks passed before my aunt spoke again. The only sounds in the house were the wall clock, the washing machine, the slow tread of her shoes when she came home from work in the late afternoon. In my heart, the feeling of doom.

At night I lay in bed flying over seas, mountains and towns, landing at the terminal where my mother farewelled us. We walked into cicada-thronged heat and caught a bus to our town.

One day, fifteen years later, I opened a Sunday newspaper to a photograph of the spa hotel where she'd worked and the story of what had happened to the women, to her. For months I too lost speech. Each breath seemed taken at knifepoint. I lost ten kilos, lost handfuls of hair, blonde hair like my mother's... *She'd pull hers back, winding it into a low bun. I'd watch her back receding in front of me as she rushed to work, her pale smock catching the sun while I ambled behind on the way to school.*

Eventually I felt a thread stitch my heart. The thread tightened over time until, one night, I felt a tug from the other side.

I took my bag from the plane's luggage rack and walked down the ramp. Rain fell heavily, turning the tarseal into black ink and glitter. An elderly woman in a headscarf stood at the entrance asking each of the woman travellers, 'Milena? Milena?' My heart thudded, but I no longer had family here. I looked back; she remained hunched like a pigeon on a power line and lit a cigarette.

A taxi swept along slick streets, pulling up outside a hostel on the square. The dark-panelled interior of my room made me feel as if I'd entered not just another place, but another time. There was no central heating, brown drapes stiff as card, and the stink of stale smoke. I pulled the chair up to the window. Rain shot through the glow of sodium lamps below. Cars sent up waves of water. I heard a cough from the next room... *Grandad coughing in the night, murmuring with my mother. Her asking him over and over to drink the medicine he hated, her voice strengthening then dissolving as if someone were turning a radio dial. Then she'd creep back into the bedroom we shared and lie down. I'd listen for her breathing, steady as a cricket in the dark.*

In the morning, I gazed down on the square. A teenager pedalled a tiny child's bike, knees bumping his chin. An ancient crust of a man, with a bush of white hair, stood holding an armful of irises. A shaft of sunlight slid from behind a cloud and his hair lit up in a halo. An equally ancient woman joined him; he held out the flowers and she cradled them like a newborn. They wandered down an alley, past a broken shop held together with strips of building paper and haphazard planks. A tree grew through the roof. A rook flew out; I stepped back. Anxiety swept over me, as I drew the drapes and sat down in the darkened room. I heard children shouting below. Coughs from next door. Sun leaked through cracks in the drapes… *blood-orange, the roses appliquéd on her coat, the lake rippling.*

I spread out the street map and the receptionist pointed where to catch the bus. 'You will like the hotel,' she said. 'People come from all over the world.' I walked across the cobbles to the far corner of the square. Nothing was how I remembered it. Rows of poles with sodden flags hanging. Shops pitted with gunfire. I felt like I was moving in a dream, like I had no body.

A woman waited at the bus shelter with a young boy. She sat folded over, one hand across her mouth as if holding in a gasp, while the boy happily swung his legs and licked an ice-block.

The bus crossed a bridge, travelling past shabby apartment blocks then meadows where horses grazed. Stop after stop, it began to fill. Two middle-aged backpackers got off before me when we reached the hotel. They trudged along the white road curving up through the pine forest to the spa where my mother had cleaned rooms. She had wanted to be a guest there. 'Just once,' she'd say, shaking out her bun like a film star. 'A room for one. No telephone calls.' Then she'd slink into our bedroom and

Grandad would call after her: 'You're a hard worker. You'll get to stay there, one day.' I shivered in the pines' filtered light.

There was a tremor in the undergrowth then a swoop of swallows squeaked overhead, feeding in mid-air. A stork appeared from behind a bush and walked past as if I were invisible. I glimpsed glassy water. A twinge; the thread pulled. I gathered wildflowers as I went: dianthus, chamomile, geraniums. The sky and the lake were the same ash grey. A swan slid toward me. I moved closer with my armful of flowers and the bird circled around, facing the mountains on the other side. I dropped the flowers onto the water. They drifted away, slowly unravelling. I had the sensation of drifting with them, then a shimmer of release. The swan floated alongside the flowers, accompanying them into the distance.

Missing

They were as startling as orchids in a paddock, especially for a Waikato farming town forty years ago. She wore a spotted white fur jacket and he a royal blue overcoat. It was a Sunday, the main street almost deserted. When she spoke to me, her words clouded the sharp air and faded into the growl of a car slowly moving past. Were there any takeaways nearby? They'd just moved to town and weren't sure what was around. 'A fish shop,' I'd replied, and I showed them the way.

Her name was Toni. She was small and slightly damaged-looking, yet her voice was strong, with tall English vowels. Iain was average-sized, with very pale eyes and sparse black lashes that made me think of a daddy long-legs. His overcoat looked a size too big as he searched through the pockets to pay.

Dusk gave everything an unreal glow: Toni's swing-cut jacket was almost phosphorescent. It had once been a snow leopard ranging across the mountains of Nepal, she told me, until her great-uncle shot it in the 1920s.

The streetlights came on as we reached the end of the main street, where it divided into two roads. Theirs was on the left. The river ran along one side, and on the other side were ten or so houses, a park with a band rotunda, then their house in the curve of the cul-de-sac. A narrow two-storey villa with broken gingerbread trim and a station wagon in the carport. We waited on the porch for Iain to find the key in those big pockets. The moon gleamed in dashes and curves across the river whose briny-mud smell enveloped us.

Iain pushed open the door and flicked the light switch. We edged down the hallway past boxes oozing clothes, books, bric-a-brac. Huge gilt-framed pictures were stacked against a closed door, faces turned away. The kitchen had an orange formica table with mismatched wooden chairs. A light bulb dangled above the table on the end of a fly-spotted cord. Toni unwrapped the fish and chips and salty steam sifted up. She turned to me and said, 'I hope there are some nicer places to eat, too. Where do you recommend?' I had only been in town a short time, but I'd spent my weekends wandering and had seen a couple of restaurants: a Chinese one at the very edge of town where the few motels petered out into farms, and a steakhouse near the police station.

Later, she instructed Iain to walk me up their unlit road to the main street. While I waited for him to go to the bathroom, I asked if they'd been in the country very long. 'Forever,' she groaned. 'In three months it'll be a year.' She dealt in antiques and curios. She said it was amazing the treasures you could find in small rural towns. Iain returned and we headed out, back past the rotunda and houses. He wore soft-soled shoes that made no sound against the footpath. If you closed your eyes, you'd think there was only one person tap-tapping along, not two.

Sometimes I go back to that town in dreams: to my flat, to my first night there. I'd woken at dawn not knowing where I was, half-hoping Mum was in the next room even though I knew she was a hundred miles away at her new job. I stood at the window and looked out at the leafless trees and the frost-glazed lawn. I was about to begin my first job in a new town, where everyone (including my flatmate) was a stranger. A shivery feeling grew. It wasn't the cold – it was the odd sensation of being alone.

I hoped to run into Iain and Toni again. I spent lunchtimes walking the town and again after work. A fortnight passed. I was starting to doubt that I would ever see them. One evening, I was sitting on a bench near the fish shop when I glimpsed a white flash in the gloom – her jacket. Iain was beside her, his blue overcoat buttoned up against the cold. I felt pinned to the bench by a pressure I couldn't name.

They'd been scouting around, Toni explained later, sitting back at their house. A second-hand dealer had Georgian sterling silver tea caddies. Iain watched Toni with a faraway expression as she described their shapes and sizes, using strange terms like *finials*. Eventually he pushed back his chair and lit a cigarette. I pictured the caddies of my childhood, which my mother had packed and unpacked so many times. I felt a pang. My father had lost and found one sharemilking job after another and we'd travelled with him. He died when I was twelve. Mum and I moved into rooms above the drapery store where she worked. The most stable time of my life; it lasted five years. The caddies had sat on the kitchen sill. They were made from beer-bottle-brown glass with white plastic screw tops, and the words TEA, COFFEE, SUGAR were stencilled on the sides.

While I waited in the hallway for Iain to put on his coat, I noticed the framed paintings had gone. The door they'd leant against was still closed, a knife-edge of light shining through the gap where it almost met the floor.

Iain suggested he drive me home – 'It's too bloody cold to walk.' He opened the driver's door and I got in the passenger's side.

I asked if he was part of Toni's antiques business. 'I help out,' he said. 'I smarten up what's shabby or broken.' His arm had brushed against me when he changed gears. He stopped at a red light and offered me a cigarette. Our foreheads nearly touched when I leant towards his lighter.

'Where do you work?' he asked.

'I'm a shorthand typist at the dairy company.'

'I've never seen shorthand,' Iain replied. 'Show me some next time.'

Next time. I lingered on those words.

'Second on the left,' I said when we reached my street. 'The block of flats. Mine's the first up the path.'

I couldn't help watching him drive away in that huge hearse-like station wagon. He took the corner so slowly it seemed as if the car were melting into the dark.

A few nights later, Iain knocked on my door. Toni was treasure-hunting out of town, he said. Would I like to go to the movies? She had the car, so we'd have to walk. It wasn't far though, and we'd warm up on the way. I don't remember what we talked about; maybe nothing. I remember the moment his hand found mine and I laced my fingers through his.

The one coffee bar in town was closing by the time we left the cinema, so we continued on to his house. This time he invited me into the lounge. Embers glowed like cats' eyes in the fireplace. It took little effort to rebuild the fire, and shadows soon flickered on the walls.

I sat on the edge of the sofa. In front of me was a round table with a copper tray that held plastic bags packed with dried leaves. Iain took the tray to another room, returning with one bag. He sat beside me and rolled a joint, held the smoke in for a beat and then let it out of his nose in a milky stream. He offered it to me. I hesitated, but I was curious too. I held in the smoke as he had. The joint went back and forth. My head grew heavy. I slipped sideways until I was lying down, my eyes closed. I felt his mouth on my neck, and the heat of the fire reaching us in waves.

I left the house early the next morning. The river had disappeared into fog, and frost starched the ground. My footsteps left prints as I crunched along. Slender, silvery tree trunks glimmered around the band rotunda and a duck waddled towards them. I turned up my collar. Everything that had made the night astonishing still clung to me like the fog to the river.

I was walking home that evening when the station wagon stopped on the other side of the road. Toni wound down the window and called my name. Did she know? My smile froze. 'Hop in,' she said. 'I've bought champagne.'

Iain didn't seem surprised when I followed Toni into the house. She told him she'd found something that would bring in a lot of money, and to fetch the rest of her things from the car. We went into the lounge. The fire cracked, leapt. I returned to the edge of the sofa. Toni's face was drawn, and when she spoke her voice seemed to echo. 'I almost fell asleep in the car,' she said. 'I've been driving for hours. I couldn't wait to get back.'

Iain came in with glasses, champagne, crackers and Camembert. The cork popped and he poured, the bubbles loud as finger-snaps. Toni stirred the fire and sparks shot up the chimney. We clinked glasses and congratulated Toni on the treasure yet to be revealed. She gently put her hand on the box she'd carried in, and stroked the lid. Iain topped up our glasses and lit a cigarette.

I wondered if I'd dreamt what happened the night before. But the pleasure was so close to the surface: the two of us moving as if caught in a storm, until the fire had dimmed and we slept pressed together.

'Anything interesting happen while I was gone?' Toni asked.

For a moment I couldn't breathe.

Iain shrugged. 'I repaired the picture frames.'

Toni touched his cheek tenderly.

'We went to the movies,' I said.

'What did you see?'

I went blank.

'*Manhattan*,' Iain replied.

Toni moved her hand from his cheek and sliced a triangle of cheese. 'Any good?'

'Not really,' he answered calmly. 'Lots of whining, not much story.'

'I think I might have had more excitement, then,' she laughed. 'Open the other bottle.'

The cork hit the ceiling and a puff of dust floated down. Toni opened the carton and carefully withdrew some kind of vase with a big gold handle. 'A mint Royal Worcester *ewer*,' she announced.

It was so ugly, my mouth dropped.

'You've probably never seen anything this beautiful before,' Toni looked at me. 'This will pay our way anywhere, or at least to Australia.'

Clay-coloured bulls were painted on the ewer, surrounded by a smeary sickly sunset, or perhaps sunrise.

'I don't think it's ever been used,' Toni said. 'The gilt is perfect and there's no crazing.' She turned the ewer upside down so we could admire the factory stamp.

Toni squeezed Iain's hand.

Suddenly I felt in the way. 'I'd better go. My flatmate's cooking tea and I said I'd be home.'

'See you,' said Toni, still looking at Iain.

Iain nodded as I walked past.

I turned at the door and saw Toni put her arm around his neck, then she reached up and kissed him.

I closed the front door quietly. I crossed the grass and stood beside the river. It was soothing to watch the water moving, moving, steadily moving while leaves and twigs circled by.

When I reached the flat, I kicked off my boots and lay on the bed. There was no tea, and my flatmate, a truckie, was already asleep after a long haul job. I can't remember what he looked like, now. I can't remember his name. There's so much that I've forgotten from back then. My father, long gone; sometimes I see his hands in dreams, swollen from labouring and weathered to a smoky brass. Only my mother's face remains, faded like a pressed flower; and theirs, Toni and Iain's.

Spring arrived and the plane trees filled with bright leaves. We'd walk through the streets when Toni was away, pretending a casual friendship. Breezes washed over us laden with fragrances: wisteria, jasmine, freesias. We meandered along the river bank and sat in the band rotunda, surrounded by a wall of cherry blossoms, looking out at the vivid grass leading down to the water. Wild gladioli had sprung up: peach, mauve. I'd rest my head on his shoulder and wish we could stay forever.

When Toni was away, I'd climb the stairs to their bedroom; when she was home, he'd knock on my window in the middle of the night. And then I didn't hear from him. After a week of lying awake as long as I could, waiting, I went to their house. The station wagon was gone. I looked in the window and the lounge was empty.

Forty years later, I was on a plane to Melbourne. I hadn't been for some time – my mother had eventually settled there, but she'd long since passed away and there was little reason to visit after that.

I was sitting in an aisle seat. There was a teenager beside me wearing headphones, asleep. I was drawn to the man next to him in the window seat, with the biker-style leather jacket and sunglasses. I glanced over several times until I was sure it was Iain.

I left the plane before him, then lagged back in the arrivals hall until he went past. He had the same even tread, although he was thinner now. I don't know why, but I'd dreamt of him recently. I had felt the past begin to move again – a leaf circling along a river.

I followed him as he went through Customs and then headed to a bar and ordered spirits. I sat nearby, wanting to approach but certain he'd forgotten me. A younger woman approached him and they embraced.

I followed them to the taxi rank and got into the cab behind theirs. 'Just follow them,' I said to the driver. 'We're together but they're having an argument.'

A grey light filtered through the window as we travelled down the freeway. The city rose in the distance like an oasis. Their cab stopped beside a park while mine was at a red light. I paid and got out.

Iain and the woman crossed the road and went into an apartment block. The doors closed behind them.

Maybe I'll come this way again, I thought. Maybe I'll sit in the park like I sat outside the fish shop, and that day in the rose gardens.

Seventeen years earlier, I'd been in Melbourne visiting Mum when she was very ill. I'd left the hospital to walk around the rose gardens. I didn't know how long Mum would live: a day, a month? And my husband and I had separated.

It was a still day, and so humid that the rows of rose beds shimmered in a heat haze. Their scent was almost overwhelming, bringing back memories of my childhood and the last house we'd lived in before moving above the drapery store. Masses of wild roses had grown across its verandah, the same red as Mum's lipstick that year. The night before we left, I'd chopped off all the roses and thrown them on the lawn. I could never explain why I'd done that. And here I was at the end of another phase of my life, immersed again in the scent of roses. I knew no-one in the city other than Mum. I'd not seen a friend in weeks. A breeze rippled through the blooms and petals floated to the ground. A familiar shivery feeling grew – I would be alone again, answering to no-one. I stood there thinking about Iain, not my husband. Why him? Perhaps because he had just disappeared.

A man in a white shirt walked past, his shirt flashing in the heat haze like Toni's jacket had flashed in the winter's gloom. The way he held his shoulders, the even tread… I began following him. As the seconds ticked by, I became convinced it was Iain. Another man strode up and he stopped. I continued past then turned to him. My heart jumped. At first I thought he didn't recognise me, but then he caught my eye. I sat on the nearest bench. At some point, which felt like forever, he came and sat beside me.

'Kat.' He touched my hand. He offered a cigarette, and our foreheads nearly touched as I bent towards his lighter. His arm brushed against me as he slipped the lighter into his pocket.

The next day, when I called his number, no answer. No answer the following day, or the one after that.

Cats and Dogs

I cleaned offices with my husband until we broke up. Then I started cleaning houses. Most people only need me for a few hours, but Mrs Shaw has me two days a week because I also keep her company. Mrs Shaw is 78. She wears navy-blue mascara and pink acrylic fingernails. When Terry the gardener comes, her eyes follow him across the lawn and her face goes soft. I can't remember when I last looked at a man like that, and I'm only 52.

Mrs Shaw's had lots of lovers. Her daughter's had lots of husbands. 'Diana takes after her father,' she says. 'Perfectly groomed, with very little sex appeal.'

Diana's my age. A psychiatrist. No children. Very prickly.

Mrs Shaw teases her about her fourth ex, who she says is the image of Omar Sharif. She'll ask, 'How's Boris Yashmak?'

'You're thinking of Boris *Pasternak*, Mum.'

'No. Your Boris, the Latvian.'

'For God's sake, his name is Poliatnioff.' (I never quite catch it.) 'His father's *Lithuanian*.'

They bicker until Diana leaves, striding past while I'm cleaning the windows or vacuuming the rugs in the hall. 'Everything alright?' she'll ask me, in a voice that says No Need To Reply.

Mrs Shaw has a beautiful home, especially the lounge which is always warm and smells of pot pourri. The walls are papered in a coarse kind of silk. There's a huge gilt-edged mirror, a velvet sofa, and armchairs covered in a print of peonies. She has a cat too: Cleo, a yellowing Persian who sits on the sofa like a puff of winter fog. Cleo's so old she can hardly walk. I pile cushions on the floor so she can get down from the sofa in stages.

Mrs Shaw and I spend a lot of time playing cards or piecing together giant jigsaws. I like the way time slows.

One day I asked her if Yashmak was Boris's middle name, or an actual word.

'No idea,' she said. 'Why don't you look it up in the dictionary?'

I did. 'The double veil worn by Muslim women in public.'

'Oh dear, I can't picture Boris in a veil,' she laughed.

'What about this word – yarpha?' I asked. 'What do you think that means?'

'Say it again, Susie.'

'Yarpha. Y-a-r-p-h-a.'

'Sounds Russian, doesn't it?'

'It *is* from Europe.'

'Latvia?'

'Scotland. Means peaty bog.'

'Well I never. Give me another.'

'Y-a-w-s. Yaws.'

'Some kind of builder's tool?'

'Button scurvy.'

And so on. Once we spent an afternoon trying to agree on the colour of the silky wallpaper. She thought it was citrine; I thought it was amber. We finally settled on golden, as in golden syrup.

All the while Cleo was sinking her claws into the velvet sofa, gazing at the garden where petunias spilled from tall urns and sparrows chirped on the lawn. Cleo's bird-catching days are long gone. She twitches and nickers, so you know she remembers, then closes her eyes as though disappointed and curls into a ball.

I finish each day making 'soup off a bone'. Mrs Shaw believes in it. A bacon hock on Mondays, a chicken on Thursdays. Then I rush to catch the bus. Usually I'm the only passenger. When it reaches the city, students pile in – crowding the aisle, arguing in foreign languages, and taking phone calls. My stop's a few doors along from a boarding house. Musty winos live there. They hang around the dairy asking for change. I can't imagine Diana the psychiatrist being able to help them. One in particular I see a lot: he has huge shocked eyes and whispers to himself. No disrespect, but I'm glad I don't clean the boarding house.

Last week I was in Mrs Shaw's downstairs bathroom when the front door opened and Diana's spiky heels struck the drying floor. They'd leave marks, and I'd have to mop it again.

'Morning Mrs Yashmak,' I heard Mrs Shaw say.

'For goodness' sake, Mum. Is Susie in?'

I gave the toilet seat a last wipe and went into the lounge.

'Ah, Susie.' Diana gave me a stare. 'I hope you're free tomorrow? I'd like you to fly to Sydney and clear out my house.'

'You're kidding, right?'

'Susie only does favours for the ancient and infirm,' her mother said.

'I'm working at the Morrison's tomorrow.'

'Can you take the day off?'

'Can't face Boris, eh?' Mrs Shaw said.

'It's *nothing* like that.'

'Why do you have to marry them? Save a lot of bother if you just took what was on offer and left it at that.'

Diana ignored her mother and said to me, 'I want you to sort through everything and give the place a good clean. Boris will pick up his belongings as agreed on this list. He's a hermit, so he won't bother you.'

'He's got lovely high cheekbones,' Mrs Shaw piped up.

The cab bowled along busy city roads, then the driver swung into a narrow street of terraced houses, pulling up in front of a shiny iron-lace fence. I got out and stood on the footpath. The stillness, the heat and the lulling perfume of a flowering tree made me feel like I was in a dream. 'Snap out of it,' I said to myself. The goodwill truck was coming at four. I went up the steps.

In the lounge were Persian rugs on black-painted floorboards. Large abstract paintings on the walls. I caught a flash of wings in the tree outside. A rainbow lorikeet joined its mate; they shrieked and made the branch shake.

Bookshelves lined the hallway. There was a formal dining room and a kitchen with slate floors, stainless steel everything, and a row of dead potted violets on the sill. The kitchen looked onto a walled courtyard with white deckchairs beneath a hazy blue-green gum tree.

I checked Diana's three-page list, to be counter-signed by Boris. It had tickboxes for everything: from sheets on the beds, to the dining table and the shell-shaped vase on top of it. On Saturday the carriers would come for the furniture, books and breakables. After that there'd be a thorough clean.

I went upstairs, stripping the double bed. Out fell a card with flowers on it; written inside was

I didn't mean what I said, I love you. With a pang in my chest, I dropped it in the bin. Then I folded the sheets, pulled off the mattress protector, folded that too. Stacked all the bedding into boxes and taped them shut. Went into the en suite, packing towels and toilet rolls and soap. Picked up the boxes and left them on the porch.

In the kitchen, I threw away anything past its use-by apart from some crackers and teabags for myself. Boxed up jars of anchovies, artichoke hearts, jam; bottles of oil, vinegar, tonic water. The truck arrived. I helped the driver with the linen boxes and he loaded up the heavy kitchen ones. Half an hour later he was gone.

Hungry, I ate a cracker – it was soft. I tossed them all into the courtyard. I'd found a brandy bottle with a few inches left in it and took a swig. A flush spread from my face to my chest. The sun had worked its way around the house, shining right into the courtyard where birds were going crazy over the crackers. I went out and sat on a deckchair. Hair had escaped from my bun, and it felt like insects were tiptoeing across my neck. The afternoon was incredibly hot and humid. Earlier, when

I'd shaken out the rugs, dust had clouded the air and stayed there.

I wondered if I should have kept the *I didn't mean what I said* card for Diana. Maybe she wasn't as together as she seemed? After all, I never knew how to show my own grief. I'd kept on good terms with my ex for the kids' sake even though they were old enough to vote, to get drunk. The last time he came to a family Christmas the kids went off to a party and we laughed through *Bad Santa*, drinking a little too much wine. The next day he went back down to his girlfriend as if nothing had happened. I just worked harder. Tried to forget the years we'd cleaned offices, chased bills, cheered on the Warriors and planned a second honeymoon in Fiji.

Flies floated in drowsy circles around the rubbish bin. Children played in the neighbouring courtyard where frangipani flowers drifted down like flakes of snow.

Something wet was pressing against my hand. For a second I didn't know where I was. I sat up, pushing the hair off my face, and saw a huge feathery dog. A man in an elegant suit, with chocolate-coloured eyes, said, 'He won't bite you. He used to live here.'

The dog rushed around the courtyard sniffing. 'You must be Susie.'

I said, 'You have lovely eyes.' Then couldn't believe I'd said it. Was I drunk? God – I was hugging the brandy bottle.

He smiled a warm easy smile. 'So do you.'

I asked if he'd like a cup of tea and went inside to make it, throwing the brandy bottle into a rubbish sack. There was only one cup left, which I hadn't sent to goodwill because it was chipped. It would have to do.

Boris leant forward to take the tea. There were silvery sparkles in his hair. I thought of my bun, half undone.

'Have you come to collect your things?' I sat down.

He looked at the house, shaking his head sadly.

I wasn't sure whether to stay where I was or start clearing the bookshelves. Then he said, 'There's a nice restaurant up the road. Would you like to join me? I'll drop Abe off on the way.' As he spoke he got to his feet, putting out his hand and pulling me up. It was so unexpected I didn't think it could really be happening. We went out onto the footpath, walking down the road with Abe trotting between us.

A crowd of fruit bats swirled overhead. I watched them swoop into a tree.

'Is this your first time in Sydney?' Boris asked.

'Yes. My husband and I had planned to travel when the kids left home. Instead we broke up.'

'It's never too late,' Boris said, leaving Abe in another courtyard. We crossed the road, continuing on dogless. His phone beeped and he stopped to read the text. I leant against an iron-lace fence. Roses wound through it: heavy blooms, more scent. He glanced up and caught me staring at him. 'Offspring!' he said. 'My daughter's going to drop by for a moment.'

The sun was setting at our backs, throwing our shadows forward. I was faint with hunger, having only eaten a cracker since the omelette on the plane. We neared a pizzeria. There was a mouthwatering smell of garlic. 'This looks nice,' I said.

'It's dirty.'

'We could get take-out, sit in a park.'

'You'll like where we're going,' he said, in Diana's no-nonsense voice, as we passed the pizzeria.

I followed him down the block and up a flight of stairs, and we were shown to a table on a roof terrace with paper lanterns overhead and oleanders growing in tubs. A waiter went past carrying plates of squid rings... There were lovely cooking smells: olive oil, rosemary. Boris ordered champagne.

I sank against the cushiony seat. The champagne was creamy and foamy and I drank it quickly. I no longer cared that I was wearing old cleaning jeans and a grubby top and had hair thick with rug-dust.

'I loved that house,' Boris said. 'Would have been worth a fortune if we'd held onto it.'

'It's just money,' I said airily – me, who had none.

His mouth went thin and he turned his glass.

'A toast?' I suggested. 'To new beginnings?'

Just then his daughter arrived wearing black short-shorts, fishnets and platform boots.

'I got the job!' she said. She flung her arms around Boris's neck, kissing him. Her happiness was magical.

'Emily's an actor,' Boris said, removing her arms.

'I blew my rent on these boots. Do you like them?'

He sighed, pulling out his wallet and handing her some money.

'Hello,' she said to me.

'This is Susie,' Boris said. 'Diana's friend.'

'Diana has a *friend*?'

'Emily!'

'I don't know if Diana has a friend,' I laughed. 'I'm just doing her a favour.'

'Well, nice to meet you.' She accepted another $20 off Boris for cab fare, blowing him a kiss and including me in her radiant smile. Men at the next table watched her go.

Boris mock-groaned, 'Do they ever grow up?'

I told him about my sons and their pierced tongues and tattoo sleeves. 'One works at Burger King,' I said. 'The other's part-owner of a bar. Bought it on Visa. It's terrifying.'

'An entrepreneur. Good for him.'

'What was Emily auditioning for?'

'A TV commercial for... pantyliners.'

This gave me the giggles – ridiculous, unstoppable giggles. Boris didn't mind; in fact he seemed relieved. A waiter brought more champagne. My hand shook when I picked up my glass. I put it down and tried a deep breath. I was tired and disorientated, yet everything felt so *good*.

After dinner Boris flagged a cab, giving the driver his address. 'It's up to you,' he said, 'but wouldn't it be nicer to stay at my place?' As if it were the most natural thing in the world, he held my hand.

This morning I went to Mrs Shaw's. She welcomed me in, wanting to hear all about Boris. 'Is he still handsome?'

'Yes.'

'Charming?'

'Very.'

'Did he ask after me?'

'Of course.'

I sat on the sofa, brushing off the ever-accumulating cat hair. For some reason Cleo put out a paw, as if she were about to make a move, and began purring.

'You're prettier than Diana,' Mrs Shaw sighed. 'You just don't know it.'

Fortunately, the lawnmower started then and she gazed over at Terry. He'd taken out the petunias, and a bright fuzz of new seedlings topped the tall urns. When the lawn was done he came over and Mrs

Shaw opened the French doors. In rushed the smell of cut grass warming in the sun.

'Just wanted a word about the hedge,' he said.

'Yes, yes, but you must have a coffee first. Susie, would you mind?'

As I went to the kitchen I caught a glimpse of her, dazzled and happy, watching Terry remove his gumboots. I heard them talking about the best way to trim the hedge and whether to plant daffodil bulbs under the magnolia. Mrs Shaw laughed a high girlish laugh, and said, 'How *lovely*, Terry.' Sunlight reached the kitchen bench, sparkling on the bowl of sugar cubes.

Where the river meets the sea

There were rustling sounds above my head where a roof should have been. A sparrow was backed into a crack in the wall, its beak opening soundlessly and then closing as its eyes clouded over. I woke angst-whipped, not sure if I'd been dreaming or remembering. I was disorientated after the 24-hour flight and the burst of heat when I'd walked out of the airport, having left my flat where icicles stabbed down from the guttering. I went straight to the rest home and Nan. She gripped my hand the way I'd gripped hers when she'd taken me up to the shops as a child. Her store of memories had long since drifted away, but some things remained wedged into a crack like that sparrow. She stared at me with a chilling fixity. Her eyes used to be soft and sultana-gold; now they were round and black. 'You called me Nan,' she whispered accusingly. I kissed her forehead and said, 'You are my Nan.' She froze. 'Reuben?' her voice quavered in the same heartbreaking lament she'd left on my voicemail a week ago. 'Reu-ben... Reu-ben.' She broke my name in two. 'All my things...' she said, 'in a skip... *crushing, crushing.*'

I fell asleep again around 2am then woke sweat-soaked and dizzy. I'd dreamt her house was spinning: I held her tight as it spun faster, then it hurtled down a shaft and thumped to a stop. We opened the door onto a garage with dank, rammed earth walls. She looked up at me and I felt her say *Take me home* even though the only actual sound was water trickling along earth.

To calm down, I opened the window above my bed. I heard a ruru's whor-whoh. The owl called again. I felt Nan's presence, a pressure in my chest.

I sat up. Now it was four in the morning; four in the afternoon back home. I was meeting Mum at the rest home at nine. I scrolled through newsfeeds on my phone and couldn't focus. The room was a sauna, same as Nan's house used to be. She left the windows closed in summer to keep out mosquitoes, kept them closed in winter to keep in the heat. Mum said all the little cottages on Nan's street had been removed, and three-storey townhouses were going up.

I heard the ruru again, further away. The

pressure in my chest intensified as the owl's call grew fainter. I dressed and left the house. Walking would help. Jet lag and sorrow had dissolved my sense of reality: I seemed to have no feet but was somehow on the move anyway. Food would help too. I hadn't eaten for almost a day. A bus neared and I stopped on the verge. Lit aquarium-blue, it turned the corner and the passengers' heads bent with the synchronised simplicity of fish. I turned left too. I headed along Chandler Avenue to Central Square and crossed to the pier. The outgoing tide had pulled the water down to the channel where the current rippled like swarms of glass eels. I went down the steps to the riverbank. There was a reek of sewage and the sour tang of Neptune's necklace clumped across rocks. Oyster-catchers dotted the mudflats, pecking for worms and crabs. I walked across the sand to a curve where the view opened out. From there, in the distance, lay the harbour's wide horizon where the river flowed to the sea and shadowy cargo ships inched along.

I thought of how glassy Nan's face had been last night. Her skin had lost pigment and the veins in her forehead looked drawn on in biro. Those newly-dark eyes gave me a shiver. Was she looking at me? Or at something I couldn't see?

I returned to the pier, passing cigarette boxes, sauce sachets and beer cans, thinking how my footsteps would disappear when the tide came in. People were sleeping under the pier, where the river never reached. I saw a lime-green sleeping bag, a floral sheet. As I reached the steps I heard a lighter click, then a plume of smoke oozed through the stair treads and over my shoes.

I spent most of my childhood at Nan's, along with Karena from next door. Mum worked and Dad was mostly away on long hauls. Nan was a collector – or pointless hoarder, as Dad said. I was bookish. I read aloud from the *Woman's Weekly* for Nan while Karena, who was my age, fossicked for buttons and grouped them by size and colour. She loved sorting Nan's things and storing them in banana boxes in the hallway. She was nervy and undersized, only coming up to my shoulder. Nan drank cups of tea – leaves, no tea bags – and knitted or crocheted as Karena sorted objects and I read out stories about royalty, babies and Nan's favourite: Lorraine Downes, Miss Universe 1983, who'd been a friend of a friend's great niece.

When the house got too stuffy, Karena and I would go down to the gully at the bottom of the road. She'd clear a patch of ground, sort leaves and branches into piles, then make floor plans with flax spears and bunches of oak leaves. We'd step carefully around the rooms she'd framed, imagining kitchens and bedrooms and lounges that opened onto decks.

I stood on the pier and watched a seagull float down and settle on a post. When it lifted up again I felt propelled by something – some echo or rhythm of another time. I pushed off the railing and returned through the Square. Office blocks lined three sides, spectral in the watery early light and haloed with gold as the sun rose. I moved on, past tourist shops with knick-knacks in the window, shuttered chemists, jewellers with bare velvet stands. I smelled bread baking but couldn't see anywhere to eat. My stomach caving in, I continued on.

I didn't know whose past I was reliving: my own or Nan's? We'd both walked this footpath countless times – it led up to the ridge where we'd rest beneath the bank's tin verandah. The once-pristine building was still there, although its windows were boarded over and only the verandah poles were left. It gave me the chills standing there. I had the eerie impression that two people were looking out of my eyes, drinking in the details: brick walls with peeling posters, bindweed winding up the ancient drainpipe whose flowers looked beautiful in the brightening light. I spun back to the river. Humidity was rising, and with it came the smell of both the river and the sea, a mix of mud and salt that made me feel homesick even as I stood right there, in my old hometown. A childhood hometown for me, a forever one for Nan. A car stopped at the lights and a snippet of music blared out... *And the mourners are all singin' as they drag you by your feet...* It drove off, but I'd been stung. Dad would arrive home from long hauls, lug in a crate of beer, then play music loud all night: Steely Dan, the Stones. In the morning, Mum would be wearing sunglasses whether or not it was sunny; long sleeves in summer, tights. My heart would beat so hard I thought I'd pass out or even die, like I'd seen a quail do when it was chased by a dog.

I crossed the road and stood outside an optometrist's. It had once been Nan's mother's boarding house and brothel. I was not part of that time, and Nan never talked about it, although her grip on my hand tightened when we walked past this building. It was Dad who'd blurted it out. I didn't know what a brothel was at ten. 'A fucken cathouse,' he'd smirked, leaving me none the wiser. I looked at glass shelves displaying rows of spectacles. Nan's round unseeing eyes, her frailty. 'How has she managed to last so long?' I asked Mum last night. 'Because she wanted to see you,' she said.

A café was open. I went in and ordered poached eggs and tea from a sleepy woman behind the counter. What had this place once been? I went blank. The radio was booming out a ten percent discount at Lighting Direct. The food arrived: white tea pot, white toast soaked in butter, two undercooked eggs whose yolks burst across the plate when I sliced into them. I ate quickly, before the yolks could congeal. A glimpse of Nan's pineapple tea cosy the same rich yellow. I wiped toast across the plate so not one smear remained. Don McLean was singing. The tea was weak and barely warm. I drank every drop. *Bye bye, Miss American Pie…*

For some reason that burst of yolks disturbed me. I left the café and continued along the road, registering all the changes with the strange double-vision sensation I couldn't explain. I wasn't sure if the time zone difference was affecting me, or whether it was my adult life coming up against my child life. I took note of everything: pigeons, nikau palms, the For Lease signs, an op shop with a naked one-legged mannequin. The fruit shop, grill rooms and womenswear had become a mini-mart, a Korean BBQ and a karaoke with private booths. The knitting shop which had once belonged to Nan now sold bric-a-brac. A taxidermied owl sat on a formica table staring out the window. My legs felt so heavy just then; I saw another time when the shop was lined with honeycomb shelving units stuffed with balls of wool, and knitted 'garments' as Nan called them, on satin-covered coat hangers.

I reached the old Dog and Family pub on the corner, which was now a vape shop displaying a two-metre high hookah. The fire escape had rotted away from the wall – just one bolt kept it from toppling off, and perhaps the weeds that had sprouted around the bolt. Karena and I had climbed the fire-escape to see all the way to where the river met the sea. The river glittered on windy days and on still ones it gleamed, a vast sheet of polished steel that hypnotised me.

I crossed the road and began walking down from the shops. Heat jellied up from the tarseal. My jeans were exactly the wrong weight, saturated with the heavy air. I wore a long-sleeved shirt – idiot. Twenty strides and I'd reach Nan's road. Shouldn't it be less now I was full-grown? Maybe fifteen? I felt giddy and steadied myself against a telegraph pole. Something was messing with my brain. Distances were warping, far and near drawing into one another. A flicker of Nan putting two fingers against her wrist and counting the beats. High blood pressure. Her face looked boiled after that awful day, and the months afterward. I pushed on to Nan's road. Her place had been a sanctuary for both Karena and I. The houses on the street had only been a foot apart and sometimes we heard Karena's parents arguing next door. We'd pretend we didn't. Nan would say 'Put on The Little Sparrow,' and I'd slip her Edith Piaf record out of its sleeve and place it on the turntable. *Non, rien de rien, non, je ne regrette rien…* Those powerful rolled 'r's sounded like a revving car. The car that knocked down Karena when she was running up to the dairy for another banana box. I'd been ambling behind in my usual dream state. Blood burst across the footpath from the gash in her head, her face turning waxy. 'Help! Help!' I'd yelled, squeezing her hand, squeezing hard – then not, in case I was forcing out more blood. The moment of knowing; then the grip of endless rewind.

I remember reading to Nan one afternoon. She had her teapot with the crocheted pineapple cosy and her cup and saucer with bluebells painted on them. It was lonely without Karena, who was still in hospital. Dad turned up and yelled at Nan, then slammed the front door and yelled some more as he went down the path. I'd shifted closer to Nan, who put her arm around me. Dad revved his Holden Monaro and tore off down the road in a bronze streak, *Your everlasting summer…* blaring out the window. 'He was meant to take you home,' Nan said, her fingers moving to check her pulse. 'Your Mum'll be expecting you for tea.'

'I'd rather stay with you,' I'd said. 'Forever.'

Not long after, maybe a year, Dad left for work as usual. Mum came home with her arm in a cast and said we were leaving town right then.

'What about Nan?' I panicked.

Mum shook her head: 'Just you and me.'

After that, I'd still come up for holidays and to read Nan the *Woman's Weekly* and listen to Piaf, those awful rolling revving 'r's giving me the shivers. Karena went to health camps now. No-one was charged for the hit and run. When I was 14, Mum remarried and we moved to Australia. I was still bookish, and my new step-dad coached rugby league. We weren't a great match, although he was always polite and never shouted. It just wasn't the same as at Nan's, where I'd been both safe and treasured.

I reached Nan's road. The old cottages had been cleared away and the framing for the townhouses was as neat as Karena's flax-spear floor plans. I had a strong sense of everything in my life being stripped back… *crushing, crushing*… Nan was too sick to visit the neighbourhood. Mum said that, over time, high blood pressure had slowly cooked Nan's brain.

I stood on the corner. The road was quiet, and out of the quietness came a *thump*. I'd thought I'd die of heart failure, like that quail. The blood congealing around Karena's head during the endless wait for an ambulance, turning burgundy, turning black.

The weight in my legs deepened. I seemed to sink rather than walk down to the gully. I knew the exact sound of his car, how its revs matched Piaf's 'r's, the flash of bronze as the Holden turned the corner – but I'd never said.

A new boardwalk curved into the bush and I went along it, past flaxes in red bloom and mānuka in pink. I saw Karena breaking off twigs to build a fireplace in her imaginary house while I picked dandelion flowers for flames.

There were trembling shadows under the old oak and a fresh rot smell of earth and leaf litter. My body ached as if it had been holding someone tight all night. Alone, with my back against the trunk and stunned by a burning sensation as if shrapnel was working its way out of my body, I noticed round eyes studying me. A ruru roosted in the fork of a cabbage tree. I felt a wave of nausea and the hair on my arms rose. Behind me, beyond the gully, an ambulance tore along, siren blaring. Then there was silence, and in that pause the owl slowly closed its eyes and blended into leafy shade. As I watched it disappear, there was a wrench deep inside of me and something painful twisted free.

Drive-by

I knew it was time when I saw my dead father standing in the doorway. He was right there, thin as a bird's wing, yet he felt far away.

My father had always been more of a suggestion than a presence. My husband had become a suggestion too – although he was still alive, in another country with another wife and further children. Occasionally we exchange polite emails.

After Dad died, my sister Maree and I weren't allowed in Mum and Dad's bedroom. His clothes remained in the closet, his guitar against the dresser. Even the newspaper that day remained where it was, with his ashtray, his cigarette butt – he'd had time for just one smoke. Afterwards, Mum only went in there for her clothes, and slept on the sofa in the lounge.

I'd sneak into the bedroom and hide beneath their bed. The air had stiffened as if it had been set with hairspray. In the stillness I'd feel my heart. It was big and heavy, like our old cat sleeping against my chest. It was sorrow, and I didn't know what to do with it. I was eight years old.

Last month, I came home with Mum's ashes. The casket was a woollen box with sage-coloured blanket stitch around the edge and an embroidered nameplate on top. I'd never seen anything like it – it was so cosy compared to the wood or marble boxes on display at the funeral directors.

The sun hadn't quite set when I drove into the carport. There were great plumes of plum-coloured clouds, the sky turning glass-green beyond them. I went inside, put the casket on the coffee table, crossed over to my daughter's bedroom and gazed in. She'd long since left home. Orchid approached and gazed in too. For years she had been more a suggestion of a cat. She was a shadow with volume, the smudge in your peripheral vision when she slunk in or out for food. Other than at feeding time she lived beneath the floorboards, where the previous tenant of the house had left her.

'What's the point of that cat?' my daughter asked repeatedly. 'She gives no love – just eats and buggers off.'

I didn't know the point of her; I only knew I

loved her, and when my daughter left home Orchid began spending more time inside.

Orchid pressed against my leg and I picked her up. I held her against my chest; her weight triggered the exact sensation I'd had when I'd gone into Mum and Dad's hairspray-stiff bedroom and slid beneath their bed.

The doors of the removal truck closed and the driver got in the cab. 'What about Dad's guitar?' I'd asked. Mum had gone dreamy, as she often used to – tipsy, I realise now. 'What about his leather jacket?' She shook her head and got in the front of the truck.

I got in the back next to Maree and the driver started the engine. Maree's eyes were glued to a comic but she wasn't turning the pages. The driver began whistling a tune I didn't recognise. Mum covered her eyes with one hand and leant against the window.

I was enraged when she zoned out, angry at her for just being a person who needed a moment when we should have had all her attention, all the time.

The truck stopped at a Give Way. A car backfired – Mum, Maree and I froze; my heart contracted into a walnut and stuck in my throat. That walnut stayed a long time. I didn't speak to Mum until Christmas, when she gave me a Pet Rock. How did she know I'd wished for exactly that? And more – she gave me two, so one would never be lonely. She'd even sewn little blankets to tuck them into their straw nests.

I was topping up my wine when I saw Dad reflected in the glass again. I turned and he was in the doorway, the same as the first time, thin as a bird's wing. He was looking at the coffee table, then he slowly disappeared. I touched Mum's casket, tracing the stitches, their tiny regular bumps, then I touched my arm. Those stitches had melted into snail trails. When the light struck at a certain angle they shone as if my arms were striped with silver.

Once I'd been queuing for a bus and a man I didn't know came up to me and said, '*Sareena!* I recognise those scars.' Kids at school asked all the time, 'Can I touch the scars?', pointing at the plum-brown lines of proud flesh worming across my arms.

The next day I drove across the city and down the motorway until I was back in the small town where my life began. Beige subdivisions sprawled across farmland. There was a beige shopping mall too, and a satellite university campus. I parked outside the old strip shops and went into a sushi bar. As I sat in the window eating tuna rolls, someone from my past trundled by. She'd been old to me when I first knew her, but now she was ancient and attached to a walker.

Aunt Sophie: famous for glueing together four sponges with chocolate ganache then coating the whole in a smooth dark glaze so the tall cake looked like a top hat. She stopped at the pedestrian crossing. Drizzle fell onto her hair and coat.

I got down off the stool and followed her across the zebra stripes.

'Aunt Sophie,' I said, overtaking her on the other side.

She stopped.

'I'm Sareena.'

Drizzle frosted her lashes, a white sheen across her eyes. 'I know no Tsarina!' she said, with the hard 't's from her first language.

'I'm Anna and Mike's eldest.'

She shook her head and trundled off.

That night, over a wine, I wished I'd shown her my scars. She might have recognised me then. How she'd pronounced my name – Tsarina – the magical twist at the beginning spinning me to a land of onion domes and sleigh rides. It had to have been her.

That old bitch, Mum called her.

Mum.

Pain shot through my heart. My scars ached.

I picked up a pencil and sketched the back of Aunt Sophie pushing her walker through the drizzle. The drizzle thickened into fog, then the fog obscured her grey bush of hair, her shoulders, lowering until it ate her like lichen eats stone, until there was only the glimmer of the walking frame, until that went too. I ripped her portrait off the pad, crunched it into a ball and threw it into the fireplace.

I'd just turned eight years old and our father was coming home. The Aunts were bringing food and Mum was making doughnuts, sweet vanilla-flavoured mouthfuls fried in sizzling oil. When the doughnuts cooled I sieved icing sugar over them. I placed three on a saucer for Maree. She was asleep, as she had asthma and had been coughing up phlegm all week. I left the saucer on her bedside table and crept out of the room

Where had Daddy been? I didn't know. There

were photos of him in the house that I'd stare at, especially the wedding photo, Mum and Dad's smiles as wide as split watermelons. Daddy was coming home from somewhere – from '*the clink*', as I'd heard Aunty Sophie hiss in the kitchen. Mum's eyes blazed, she made the 'zip your lips' gesture and told Aunt Sophie to pass her the measuring cup.

I waited on the footpath, wearing my new checked pinafore with piping around the bodice. It was comforting running my finger along the raised satiny line, back and forth, back and forth, waiting at the gate. The neighbour's dog watched from behind his fence. The two of us were waiting and time was so slow. The air was hot and syrupy. Birds swirled overhead. The dog gruffled and lay with his muzzle resting on his outstretched legs. Daddy. I felt shy and wished Maree was waiting with me.

Eventually Uncle Andy's car turned the corner, with Daddy in the passenger seat. My heart ballooned. I jumped up and down, waving. The car slid to a stop, then he got out and lifted me up to the sky. '*Sareena, Sareena.*' He hugged me so tight I felt like a foot squashed into a too-small shoe.

He put me down and I think he was crying.

I've never drawn this. I've never drawn him upset, the squashed foot feeling, my heart about to burst.

I want to forget many things. I want to forget everything that came later, yet keep this one moment, to breathe it into my being until it's a curl of fur that starts breathing too.

Daddy just stood where he was with his sad, watery eyes. I held his hand and led him toward the house, where everyone was waiting to surprise him beneath streamers and strings of balloons.

The sun shone on my face as I stood at the ranchslider in Mum's room at the rest home. It was warm and peaceful, and Mum was asleep; I listened to her breathing and to the wall clock's regular tock reminding me of my footsteps just before falling, falling onto the carpark's tarseal in the rest home quiet. A young magnolia tree was flowering to my right. It was hypnotic watching bees approach, rummage amongst the yellow stamens, then lift off and circle away.

Bang! My heart stopped. A bird had smacked against the ranchslider and plopped onto the balcony. I turned to Mum – the noise hadn't woken her – then

I stepped outside. The bees were buzz-saw loud and the magnolia smelt sickly. I felt giddy when I knelt down. The bird's body was still, with one wing raised crookedly. Then its foot quivered. The bird jerked the broken-looking wing into position and stood. A moment later it flew. I watched it sail up around the corner of the building towards the sun.

I went back inside. Mum's eyes were wide and fixed and her mouth was slightly open. She looked as if she'd just witnessed something amazing.

On that long-ago day when Dad returned, the glass shards caught Maree on the forehead. She told kids she'd been attacked by a dog. Really, she'd staggered to Mum and Dad's bedroom and clung onto the door handle, breathing her asthma wheeze. Mum, Dad and I had turned to her.

Bang! The window burst and Dad thumped onto the bed, my ears roared as red spread out. Mum's face twisted. She screamed but I couldn't hear her. I looked down: my arms had split open.

Maree and I buried Mum's woollen casket in Dad's grave. After that, I never saw him again.

Growing

All the rest home doors have name tags. Mum's has a typo: *Irina*. Although Irena isn't her born name – only she knows what that is, and she's never told, never discussed the war. Says she was born the day she reached Wellington harbour with papers stating she was a ten-year-old Polish orphan. Dad said not to ask about the European years, and my brother and I never did. Now they've both died and there's just me and Mum, and she's in a rest home with a misspelled name on her door.

Dad emigrated from England after the war. He'd been in the air force and had 'seen things,' he said. That's as far as his war stories went. My brother and I didn't give it much thought; we had a pretty idyllic childhood, ducking and diving around them both. Basketball hoops and swingball, a rope strung between the pear and apple trees for a tennis net. Mum spoke to us softly in English and patted the tops of our heads. When Dad was home from work he'd be painting the roof or the house, or pruning trees with his leather-bound wireless tuned in to cricket or rugby. He intended to visit England again one day, but never did. He died of a heart attack when I was 34 and my brother 32. We grew up anchored by the seasons. In spring, Mum planted marigolds and camomile out front and potatoes, carrots and lettuce in the vegetable garden. She sowed seeds for summer flowers – alyssum, cosmos, sweet peas. Sweet peas were my favourite. It was lovely picking the stems and parcelling them out to neighbours in newspaper triangles. When the seedpods clacked in the breeze and the leaves turned gold, Mum chopped up the plants and dug them into the soil as manure. The only time I smell in dreams is when a jasmine-orange sweet pea fragrance wakes me. I feel such a strong presence, I'm not sure if someone is in the room or if it's a wandering sense memory.

While Dad was at work, Mum cleaned, baked, knitted, sewed and cooked. When she wasn't using her hands, a tremor ran through them; if she caught me noticing, she'd find something to peel or chop or wash. The tremor is still there, although the things she can do to disguise it have greatly diminished. She's almost blind now, and can only knit scarves. I bought her large gauge needles and brilliant-coloured yarns. Every week I bring more yarn and watch her knit more scarves. Sometimes I just want to sit and hold her hands, but I never do. I pat the top of the head like she used to pat my brother and me.

If it's nice weather, we walk around the rest home's gardens. I push her wheelchair past roses, daphne and lavender. I break off blooms so she can take them to her room. There are beautiful vegetable gardens too. Dill on a hot day and tomatoes, their scent taking us back to the family home. In the afternoons, caregivers set up a hotplate in the lounge and make batches of pikelets or corn fritters, because these cooking smells stir the residents' memories. Today Mum and I sat in the lounge, her knitting needles whisking, another scarf lengthening, and I asked myself what smells will trigger memories for me when I'm old and in a rest home. Sweet peas?

I stopped at the garden centre on the way home and bought sacks of compost and packets of the seeds we used to grow: Cupani, Blue Danube and ballerina-pink Princess Juliana. I thought of something one of the other Polish refugees had told me in confidence years before.

She said they'd found Mum in Siberia. They'd been trudging through woods and then vast open plains when someone glimpsed pale blue eyes staring from the edge of a juniper bush. The blue-eyed creature was more bird's nest than child: hair a clump of knots and twigs, grass and leaves stuck to mud-caked clothes. 'Who do you belong to?' they asked. The silent child trembled. The Poles saw shingle roofs up a dirt track to the left. As they neared, the stench of rotting meat threw up a kind of wall. Some stopped right there between the juniper bush and the village, while a few others struggled on up the track, hands held across their faces. A pit had been dug alongside a barn and it was filled with bodies, stiff legs and arms reaching out of the soil. The people had been lined up and shot in the back. Their vegetable gardens had been trampled by horses, doors broken off their log houses and human shit left on doorsteps. No animals were left, not even a chicken – just clouds of flies whirring loud as tinnitus. Sun shot through strings of sweet peas blooming along the edge of a henhouse. The Poles tore off handfuls of the fragrant flowers and held them to their noses as they returned down the track. Old Tomasz hoisted the blue-eyed child onto his back. She weighed next to nothing, he said. A sack of feathers. When they finally reached the train that would take the children to a Persian orphanage, he said she was his granddaughter Irena.

'Age?'

'Eight years,' he guessed.

'Is she deaf?'

'She is starving.' Old Tomasz patted her on top of the head. He'd borne this sack of feathers for weeks, and now she would travel into the future carrying his dead wife's name.

I opened the packets of seeds and let them spill onto a plate. They looked like muddy pearls. I knew what to do – I'd helped Mum many times. I nicked each seed and ran a nail file across them. I lined a Tupperware container with a damp paper towel, lay down the seeds and closed the lid. In the morning the seeds had swollen, and that afternoon each one had a white root poking out.

I dug a trench alongside my garage and worked a layer of compost into the soil. I was reminded of

Mum and I baking scones, cutting cold butter into flour until the pieces were small enough to rub in. I put aside the spade and knelt down to rub the clods of earth into the compost, then I stepped into the trench and treaded out air pockets. How like a burial planting seeds is: the hole, the offering, the covering over. I jumped out and added a layer of topsoil, then another layer of compost. Would Mum live long enough to smell these flowers? I jabbed holes in the ground with the end of a pencil, dropped the seeds and covered them over.

The next morning, I bought more packets of seeds and took them to a jeweller in the mall. He agreed to string them together with a knot in between each one, just like a string of pearls.

I took them to Mum the following day. 'Do you recognise these?' I asked. She put down her knitting and I closed her hand around the string. 'Sweet peas,' she said. She slowly slipped seed after seed through her fingers, then chanted in a low voice in a language I'd never heard before.

When I drove home, I realised I should have recorded Mum on my phone. Surely I could have found someone who'd understand what she'd said?

That night, Mum died in her sleep. The chaplain tried to comfort me by saying she'd gone home – as if I knew where that was.

Soon after, the sweet peas by the garage began to bloom.

I still wake, sometimes, to that rich jasmine-orange fragrance. Now I know who's there.

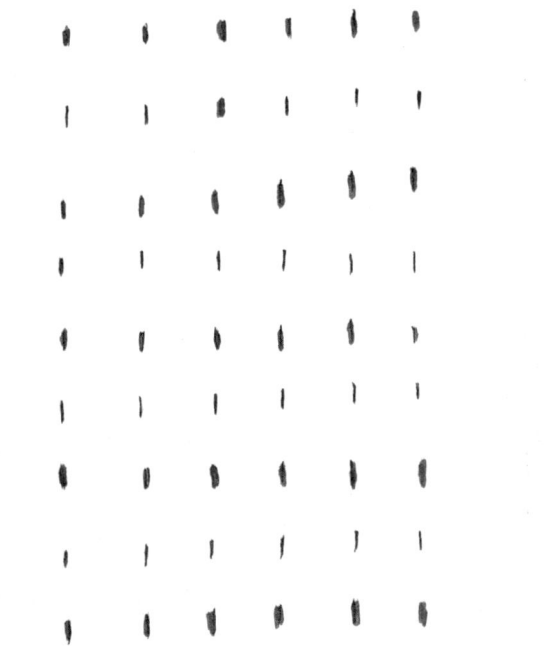

ACKNOWLEDGEMENTS

Thank you Emma Dai'an Wright for choosing *Hailman*, for being a wonderful editor, and for creating magical cover art. Thank you Mary-Jane Holmes and Lynne Price for wise feedback. Heartfelt thanks to my family and friends who generously support my writing, including fellow travellers Frankie McMillan and Zoë Meager; and thank you, always, Lawrence, Jack and Jane.

Thanks also to the editors of these publications and websites where some of the stories have appeared: *Landfall, ReadingRoom, Short Fiction Journal, takahē, Turbine|Kapohau* and *An Encounter in the Global Village: Selected Stories from the 14th International Conference on the Short Story in English* anthology (Shanghai: East China Normal University Press, 2016).

ABOUT THE AUTHOR

Leanne Radojkovich's debut short story collection *First fox* was published by The Emma Press in 2017. Her work has been anthologised in *Bonsai: Best small stories from Aotearoa New Zealand* and the forthcoming *Best Small Fictions 2021*.

In 2018 she won the Graeme Lay Short Story Competition and was a finalist in the Anton Chekhov Prize for Very Short Fiction. She was longlisted for the 2020 Short Fiction/University of Essex Prize and shortlisted for the 2020 Sargeson Prize.

Leanne holds a Master of Creative Writing (First Class Honours) from AUT Auckland University of Technology. She has Dalmatian heritage and was born in Kirikiriroa Hamilton. She now lives in Tāmaki Makaurau Auckland, where she works as a librarian.

@linedealer

ABOUT THE EMMA PRESS

small press, big dreams

ʘʓʚʘ

The Emma Press is an independent publishing house based in the Jewellery Quarter, Birmingham, UK. It was founded in 2012 by Emma Dai'an Wright and specialises in poetry, short fiction and children's books.

The Emma Press has been shortlisted for the Michael Marks Award for Poetry Pamphlet Publishers in 2014, 2015, 2016, 2018 and 2020, winning in 2016. Moon Juice, a poetry collection by Kate Wakeling for children aged 8+, won the 2017 CLiPPA.

In 2020 The Emma Press received funding from Arts Council England's Elevate programme, developed to enhance the diversity of the arts and cultural sector by strengthening the resilience of diverse-led organisations.

The Emma Press is passionate about publishing literature which is welcoming and accessible.

Visit our website and find out more about our books here:

Website: theemmapress.com
Facebook @theemmapress
Twitter @theemmapress
Instagram @theemmapress